Ladybird First Favourite Tales

Cinderella

BASED ON A TRADITIONAL FOLK TALE

retold by Ronne Randall ★ illustrated by Ailie Busby

Once there was a beautiful girl called Cinderella, who lived with her mean stepmother and stepsisters.

The stepsisters wore fancy ribbons and laces,
but they both had such UGLY faces.
Cinderella was gentle and sweet, but she
had to wear rags and clogs on her feet.

One day, a note came from the palace.

"The prince is having a ball," said the stepmother, "and he has invited all the young ladies in the kingdom!"

Cinderella's stepsisters were very excited.
"Help us get dressed in our very best,"
they squawked at Cinderella.

On the day of the ball, Cinderella helped her stepsisters primp and preen.

They rode off in a carriage with their heads held high. Cinderella watched and waved, then sat down to cry.

"How I wish I could go to the ball," Cinderella wept.

Suddenly, with a flash of light and a whoosh of air, a kind old lady was standing there!

"Who are you?" Cinderella cried.
"I'm your fairy godmother," the woman replied.
"You shall go to the ball!"

Then, with some flicks of her wand and a few magic words, the most amazing things occurred!

Is this all for me?

The fairy godmother turned a pumpkin into a coach...

...six mice into six fine horses, and a rat into a handsome carriage driver. Six lizards became six footmen in green coats.

"Now for the best part," said the fairy godmother, flicking her wand up and down.

Cinderella's rags became a beautiful gown! She shimmered with jewels and on her feet were two glass slippers, dainty and neat.

"Have a good time at the ball!" her fairy godmother
called. "But be back before midnight – that's when
the magic will end!"

Everyone at the ball wondered who the lovely girl was. Even her stepsisters didn't recognize Cinderella.

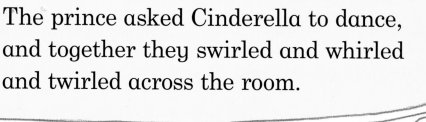

The prince asked Cinderella to dance, and together they swirled and whirled and twirled across the room.

To Cinderella's great delight, the prince danced only with her all night. Cinderella was having such fun that she forgot all about her promise to her fairy godmother...

Suddenly, the clock struck twelve!

Cinderella ran out of the palace and down the stairs. The prince ran after her, but he couldn't see his princess. There was only a girl wearing rags.

Then the prince saw something gleaming by his feet.

"It's her glass slipper!" he said. "I know what I'll do. I'll search the kingdom through and through to find the girl whose foot fits this shoe."

The prince visited every house in the kingdom. "I will marry the girl who can fit into this slipper," he told everyone.

Both of Cinderella's stepsisters tried. The first one's feet were MUCH too wide. She wouldn't be the prince's bride!

The second stepsister's feet were TOO fat and hairy.

Very scary!

The prince was about to leave when he heard
a voice, gentle and shy, say: "Please may I try?"

The stepsisters laughed and called out, "YOU?!"
But the prince said, "Yes, please do."

Of course, the slipper fitted Cinderella perfectly!

Suddenly, Cinderella's fairy godmother appeared once more. With a flick of her wand, Cinderella wore a beautiful ball gown.

The prince took Cinderella into his arms
and said, "Will you be my bride?"
"Yes, I will," Cinderella replied.

So they were married, and lived happily ever after.

Collect the other books in the series

9781409306283

9781409309574

9781409306306

9781409309550

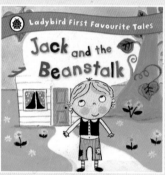

9781409309598

9781409309581

9781409306320

9781409306313

9781409306337